MYSTERIOUS MORPHO

Agaricus.

For Elmo and Sarah.
Special thanks to Max Fiedler
and Rumi Benecke – Lomp

LITTLE TIGER PRESS LTD,
an imprint of the Little Tiger Group
1 The Coda Centre
189 Munster Road
London SW6 6AW
www.littletiger.co.uk

First published in Great Britain 2017
This edition published 2018
Text and illustrations copyright © Lomp 2017
Lomp has asserted his right to be identified
as the author and illustrator of this work under the
Copyright, Designs and Patents Act, 1988
A CIP catalogue record for this book is available
from the British Library

All rights reserved • ISBN 978-1-84869-680-8

Printed in China
LTP/1400/1828/0417
10 9 8 7 6 5 4 3 2 1

WILFRED AND OLBERT's TOTALLY WILD CHASE

Written and illustrated by Lomp

LITTLE TIGER
LONDON

One fine morning Wilfred Wiseman and Olbert Oddbottom, two famous animal explorers, are having a cup of tea . . .

. . . when a strange visitor flies in through the window and lands on Olbert's rather large nose. Could it be a undiscovered species?

Zoom! The speedboat rushes off! Will chases the butterfly down the river and out to sea . . .

The butterfly swims on.
But Ollie has taken Will's diving gear.
Uh-oh! What should Will do?

Aha! Will has got an extendable straw. The chase continues through a colourful coral reef . . .

Will and Ollie flee the shark and find themselves on a hot beach that leads to a dry desert . . .

... and across a wild grassland.
Surely it's time for this silly race to stop!

Thump! The balloon crashes in an icy land.
The wind must have taken them very far.

SEAGULL

ARCTIC FOX

ARCTIC HARE

POLAR BEAR

WALRUS

PUFFIN

I'm sorry I crashed your balloon.

I am just glad you are ok.

Let's study the butterfly and enter the prize together. I'm tired of fighting.

Me too. I think it flew this way.

PENGUIN

SEAL

Do you think this ice will hold us?

Oh yes. It's rock solid!

But I think I heard a crack.

Hm. Then maybe we should…

AAAH!!

Ollie!

…RUN!

Ollie and Will scramble up the tree trunk . . .

Yes! Ollie and Will have done it! Standing in front of them is their magnificent butterfly – and it doesn't fly away!

Will and Ollie grow back to full size and the butterfly flies off. Luckily, they have everything they need to enter the prize and so they head home.

Two weeks later, the winners of The Nature Discovery Prize are announced.
And who do you think they are?

Hooray for Will and Ollie! They worked together, found the butterfly and won the prize. What a great adventure!

Oh, and here are the solutions to the puzzles. Did you solve them all?

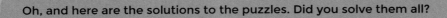

Psst! There are three new undiscovered animals in the book. Can you find them? What will you call them?

More totally wild books from Little Tiger Press!

THERE'S NO SUCH THING AS A SNAPPENPOOP
Jeanne Willis · Matt Saunders

FAIRY TALE PETS
TRACEY CORDEROY · JORGE MARTÍN

THE CURIOUS CASE of the Missing MAMMOTH
Packed with facts and flaps!
ELLIE AND HATTIE

HIBERNATION HOTEL
John Kelly · Laura Brenlla

NIBBLES The BOOK Monster
EMMA YARLETT

Hyde and Squeak
FIONA ROSS

For information regarding any of the above titles or for our catalogue,
please contact us: Little Tiger Press, 1 The Coda Centre,
189 Munster Road, London SW6 6AW · Tel: 020 7385 6333
E-mail: contact@littletiger.co.uk · www.littletiger.co.uk

For William S, who at age 2 listened to
my very first story and said, "Again!" – L.R.

For the three little monsters,
Elizabeth, Sophie and Adam! – M.C.

First published 2017 by Macmillan Children's Books
an imprint of Pan Macmillan
20 New Wharf Road, London N1 9RR
Associated companies throughout the world
www.panmacmillan.com

ISBN: 978-1-4472-8668-4 (HB)
ISBN: 978-1-4472-8670-7 (PB)

1 3 5 7 9 8 6 4 2

A CIP catalogue record for this book is
available from the British Library.

Printed in China

Jake Bakes a MONSTER CAKE

LUCY ROWLAND MARK CHAMBERS

MACMILLAN CHILDREN'S BOOKS

One Saturday, Jake decided to bake
A cake for his friend's birthday tea.

He said, "What a treat!
Sam *loves* something sweet,
And my friends can help make it with me."

But you see it was tricky, Jake's friends were so picky,
Their plans were quite different to Jake's.

They liked juicy bugs
And fat slimy slugs
To flavour their favourite cakes.

That day Monster Tor arrived at Jake's door
And Ben walked behind with young Fred.

Tilly was late
But she rushed through the gate.
"It's time to get started," Jake said.

"What time do you call this?"

They hurried inside, and with aprons all tied,
Jake showed them the recipe book.

But Tor laughed with Tilly,
"Oh Jake, don't be silly!
We don't need *instructions* to cook!"

She grabbed smelly eggs,
   eight spidery legs,
Five ants, some old pants -
   about ten.

"Give them back!"

She whisked them
and whirred them,

She mixed them
and stirred them,

Then handed the
bowl on to Ben.

Ben shouted, "My turn!" And he threw in a worm.
He laughed, "It says here to add LIME!

Jake started to mutter, "But what about butter?
Perhaps some more sugar?" he tried.

Fred thought for a minute,
Then threw a SLUG in it.
"But these are so gooey!" he cried.

Tilly said, "Please can I add in some cheese?
I promise it's really delicious!

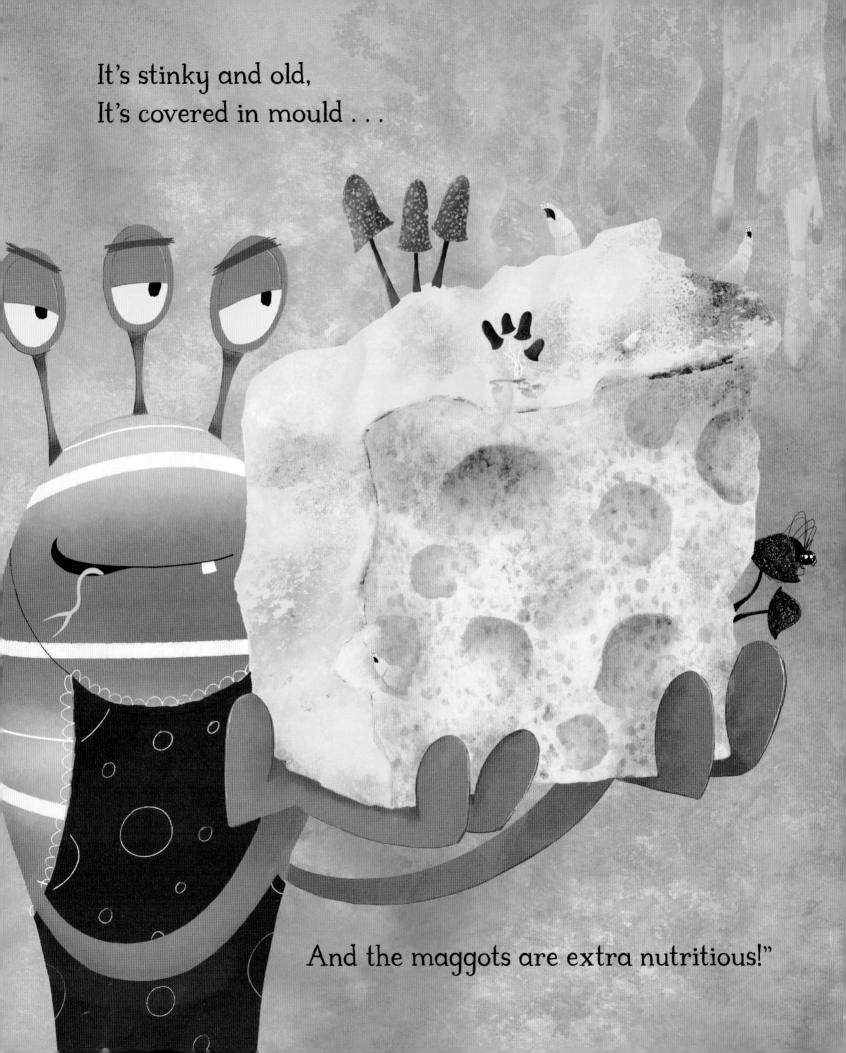

It's stinky and old,
It's covered in mould . . .

And the maggots are extra nutritious!"

But Jake said, "Enough! Now, I'll have to get tough.
You'll ruin our present for Sam!"

Then a splash of the paste
Landed right on Jake's face . . .

"YUM!
What a good
baker I am!"

With the mixture cooked through,
Jake called the whole crew
To carry the *huge* bake outside.

SAM'S HOUSE

But then in a muddle,
Jake slipped in a puddle . . .

"Uh-oh!"

And groaned as he watched the cake slide!

Sam opened his door as the cake hit the floor.
It fell with a SPLAT to the ground.

"Happy birthday," sobbed Jake,
While Sam stared at the cake,
And nobody else made a sound.

"I'm sorry," Jake cried,
his eyes open wide,
Sam frowned and he
puffed out his chest.

He turned towards Jake,
"When it comes to good cake . . .

"MUD PIE is quite simply the BEST!"

Add your
own stinky egg
smells with the
scratch 'n' sniff
stickers!

Can you find the bone hidden
on each double page?